Zoey

AND

SASSAFRAS

THE POD AND THE BOG

THE INNOVATION PRESS

READ THE REST OF THE SERIES

for activities and more visit
ZOEYANDSASSAFRAS.COM

TABLE OF CONTENTS

FOR NICOLA AND JO — ML
FOR GOOSE AND BUBS — AC

Audience: Grades K-5.
LCCN 2017918473
ISBN 9781943147373; ISBN 9781943147380; ISBN 9781943147397; ISBN: 9781943147458

Text copyright 2018 by Asia Citro
Illustrations copyright 2018 by Marion Lindsay
Journal entries handwritten by S. Citro

Published by The Innovation Press
1001 4th Avenue, Suite 3200 Seattle, WA 98154
www.theinnovationpress.com

Printed and bound by Worzalla
Production Date: March 2018 | Plant Location: Stevens Point, Wisconsin

Cover design by Nicole LaRue | Book layout by Kerry Ellis

PROLOGUE

These days my cat Sassafras and I are always desperately hoping we'll hear our barn doorbell.

I know most people are excited to hear their doorbell ring. It might mean a present or package delivery, or a friend showing up to play. But our doorbell is even more exciting than that. Because it's a magic doorbell. When it rings, it means there's a magical animal waiting outside our barn. A magical animal who needs our help.

My mom's been helping them basically her whole life. And now I get to help, too . . .

CHAPTER 1
BEDTIME

I steadied my ruler in the soil next to my pea plant. "Whoa! It's up to 8 inches now, Sassafras." I wrote down the date and the new height in my science journal.

Sassafras touched his nose to the plant and meowed.

"I know! I'm totally surprised too. When Clara asked me what would happen if we used a marker to color on all the pea plant leaves, I thought for sure the pea plant would stop growing or maybe even

die." I turned my science journal toward Sassafras, and he gave it a sniff. "I can't wait to surprise her with it when she comes over to play again."

Mom popped her head in. "Ready to read, Zoey?"

"Yes!" I yelped and hopped up from my desk.

"Pajamas and cap?"

"Check!"

"Teeth brushed?"

"Check!"

"Pea plant measured?"

"Check! And look—it's still growing." I handed Mom my journal.

Mom took it and looked it over. "Well done! And you know what I'm going to ask next, right?"

I nodded eagerly. "'What other questions do you have now?' I have a bunch! Like what happens if I color the top *and* the bottom of the leaf? And what if I try a different color on each plant? Will some colors grow better? Oh! And what about different kinds of plants? Is it just pea plants that keep growing with marker on their leaves?"

Mom patted my head and smiled. "All excellent questions! But since it's time for bed, we'll have to work on them tomorrow. Shall I begin our story?"

Sassafras started purring and hustled over to my lap. I giggled as I put away my science journal.

Mom got cozy at the foot of my bed and opened the book. "Now where were we?"

"We were right at the part where—"

Sassafras leaped out of my lap and held very still with his ears pointing outside.

I looked at Mom. "Did you hear something? Was that . . . ?"

It was unmistakable this time. That was definitely the sound of the barn doorbell!

CHAPTER 2
NIGHTTIME  VISITOR

Sassafras chattered and ran to my bedroom door and back. I clasped my hands together and gave Mom my sweetest smile. "Pleeeease, can I go?"

Mom looked at her watch and sighed. "OK, but take a flashlight and come back right away. If it's something serious, I can take over for you. It's late and you need your sleep."

I leaped out of bed and ran for the door, calling out over my shoulder, "Thank you, thank you, thank you! I promise we'll be right back!"

I grabbed a flashlight out of the kitchen drawer and slipped on my shoes, and then Sassafras and I bolted across the yard to the barn. My heart was pounding not just from running, but also from the excitement of meeting a new magical creature.

"Who do you think it will be this time, Sassafras?" I panted.

Sassafras stopped running and leaped into the air. Then he chewed and swallowed.

"Ew, Sass! Did you just eat a bug?"

"Meow!" he answered triumphantly.

I shook my head disapprovingly as I opened the door. "Remember, Sassafras. No trying to eat our magical friends. Even if they are very buglike. It's just not polite."

We ran through the barn to the back door. The moment of truth! I took a steadying breath and opened the door.

Just above the ground was a large glowing rainbow . . . stone? "Wowww!" I knelt down and reached out a finger. It was like a merhorse stone, but the size of a soccer ball. That familiar shimmering rainbow light meant one thing: whatever this was, it was definitely magical. Sassafras stood frozen next to me. His eyes were like big saucers.

"Ahem! A little help, please? This thing is really heavy!" called a small voice. A small voice I knew.

"PIP!!!!" I shrieked. Perhaps a little too loudly. Pip stumbled backward, and I managed to grab the rainbow stone just before it hit the ground. Pip was the magical talking frog who had started it all. My mom found him hurt badly in the forest when she was my age and nursed him back to health. He was one of my favorite magical creatures—he always managed to make me laugh.

"Sheesh, Zoey! You scared me! Your

giant human voice can be quite startling, you know." Pip brushed himself off just in time to have a giant furry Sassafras head crash into him. This time he did fall over, and we both laughed.

"I guess you both have missed me, yes?"

"Absolutely!" I grinned as I helped Pip back to his feet.

I held out the glowing stone. "What is it? Where did you find it? And is something wrong with this, um, rainbow stone?"

"Ah, great questions! I would expect nothing less from you. Let's start at the beginning. That is most definitely not a stone. It is a seed pod from some kind of magical plant."

I slowly rolled it between my hands. "A magical seed pod? That is so cool."

Pip nodded in agreement. "I was just getting ready for bed and was all cozy when I heard an enormous *THUD* outside my home. Of course I had to go see what it was! When I got outside, this was lying there on the ground. My best guess is that some sort of flying magical creature was trying to steal it for food and accidentally

dropped it."

Sassafras watched as I poked and fiddled with the pod. "See, Sassafras? It's kind of like our pea plant. Only instead of a long seed pod, this one is round and a lot bigger. I wonder if the seeds inside look like peas. What color do you think the seeds are? Argh, this thing is impossible to open!"

"Should we be trying to get it open? I wasn't sure what to do, but I figured I shouldn't just leave it at my house," Pip explained.

"Oh, good point! Hmmm, let's see . . . it's from some sort of magical plant, so

should we try to figure out which one first? Have you seen pods like this before, Pip?"

"That's the thing. I haven't ever seen one like this. Do you think it's a really rare kind of plant? What if it's endangered?"

I put my hand to my mouth. "What if it's the last of its kind? We've got to get it back to where it belongs! And we need to keep it super safe until then."

"That sounds like a good plan. Since I've never seen it, I think it must be from

pretty far . . ." Pip stopped and stretched and gave a big yawn. "Um, pretty far away." And then he yawned again.

And then Sassafras yawned.

And then I heard my mom calling me from the house.

I rubbed my eyes a little. "OK, I think we are all pretty tired. This should be safe in the barn tonight. Can we meet first thing tomorrow to get started on a plan?"

Pip nodded sleepily. I made a little blanket nest on a chair in the barn and carefully placed the glowing seed pod in the middle.

Mom called again.

"Good night, Pip!" I kissed him on the head, and Sassafras licked him on the cheek.

"Blech." Pip wiped off our kisses. But he was smiling. "I'll see you two tomorrow!"

CHAPTER 3
ALL ABOUT PLANTS

The next morning, Mom, Sassafras, and I crowded around the glowing seed pod. The pod continued the beautiful shimmering cycle we'd seen the night before: red slowly and gracefully blended into orange, then changed to yellow, and so on until it had gone through all the rainbow colors and started over again.

"I could stare at this all day," Mom said finally.

"Me too! But we should work on getting

it back to the right place. I don't know if keeping it here could hurt it somehow. I don't want anything bad to happen to it."

Mom patted my head. "So responsible! You're right." Mom grabbed one of her old science journals and flipped it open. "Let's see here . . . Pip was right about magical plants being rare. I've heard that from several magical creatures. The only magical plant I've ever seen was this one." Mom turned the journal around so I could see.

"Are those furry purple . . . fruits?" I reached a finger out to touch the photo. "Ooh, they're so soft!"

Every time we take a photo of

something magical, the photo keeps a bit of magic. So even though it was just a photo of a giant purple plant, I could feel the fur on the fruits.

"Yep, they are! But the seeds from that plant are inside those fruits, not seed pods. So this pod is definitely a different species."

"How are we going to figure out where it came from?" I asked.

Mom raised an eyebrow at me.

"Umm, maybe we could read? About real plants? To see if there are any that are similar?"

Mom motioned with her hand to keep going.

"And, uhhh, we could . . . look at maps? To see the different sorts of places around here a plant might grow?"

Mom grinned. "You have some great ideas to get you started. Unfortunately, I have a ton of work. Do you think you and Sassafras can figure it out? I'll be inside if you need me . . ."

I popped my Thinking Goggles on my head and nodded confidently. "Go work. We've got this."

CHAPTER 4
FROM WHERE?

I set a big serious-looking book down on the table next to the seed pod. "OK Sassafras, I'm going to read about different kinds of seeds in this botany book. Maybe there's a real-life seed pod that looks like this. And then we can get a hint about where this one might grow!"

Sassafras ignored me and instead sniffed all around the seed pod. He reached out a paw and bopped it softly. Then harder. The seed pod rolled away from him, then bonked into the wall and rolled straight back at him. Sassafras hissed and jumped backward with his tail puffed up.

I caught the seed ball before it rolled off the table and laughed. I tapped him gently on the nose with one finger. "Why don't you try and stay out of trouble while I read?"

Sassafras grumbled and jumped down from the table.

While Sassafras explored spider webs in the corners of the barn, I read about seed pods and fruit seeds and flying seeds and dangling seeds called catkins (I liked saying that word because it reminded me of cats). But nothing sounded at all like our rainbow pod.

"Ugh, Sassafras. Reading is not working. Now what do I do?"

Sassafras gave a little meow and began pacing the barn.

I joined him and tapped my Thinking Goggles. It made a fun sound, so I started tapping out a little beat. That made me want to hum. And the humming quickly turned into a little song:

Oh seed pod, seed pod,
At your colors we are awed.

I paused at the table. Wait a second. Was the seam getting bigger on the seed pod? Maybe my eyes were playing tricks on me. I shrugged and kept singing:

This is really kind of odd.

Then I jumped a little. The seam definitely looked bigger. Whoa. I scrambled to come up with more words to the song:

At your surface, my cat pawed.

And a magic creature clawed.
I think you live somewhere abroad.
If I knew where, I would APPLAUD!

All at once, the two halves of the seed pod swung apart.

We peered inside at a couple dozen shiny black seeds as perfectly round and about the same size as bouncy balls. I reached in and pulled out a handful.

Sassafras and I silently stared. Then I felt a frog on my head.

"WHOA, ZOEY! IT'S OPEN!" Pip exclaimed. He jumped down to my wrist and touched a seed with a webbed hand. "You left the barn door open so I just let myself in. What happened?"

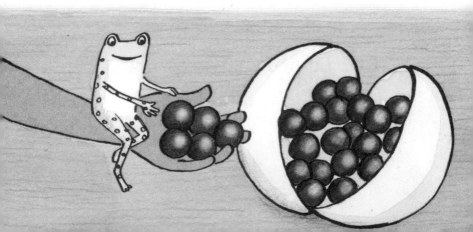

"I think the pod liked my singing? I kept going, and it popped open!"

Just then Mom walked in with a sandwich. "Do I hear my favorite frog?"

Pip hopped over to Mom, and we told her everything we'd figured out so far.

"Well, this certainly makes things interesting," she said. "You couldn't figure out any hints on where the seed pod might grow from reading. Can you think of something other than reading that we could try?"

I tapped my trusty Thinking Goggles. "Do you think we could–? I mean, would it be safe to use some of the seeds in an experiment?"

"Aha! Good thinking," said Mom. "That's what I would try next. We have a good number of seeds. What sort of experiment do you have in mind?"

Once I explained my idea to Mom, it was time to get to work.

CHAPTER 5
EXPERIMENT!

I dashed back into the barn. Sassafras lay sleeping with Pip curled up on top of him. I tossed my science journal onto the table. I'd meant to do it quietly, but it made a big slamming noise instead. Sassafras jumped up, launching Pip into the air.

"Aaaaaaahhhhh!" yelled Pip as he flew across the room.

Whoops.

"Sorry, guys!"

"Now that I'm wide awake," said Pip as

he brushed himself off, "you might as well tell me what you've figured out."

"I made a list of all the places around here that I thought the plant might grow. Mom had a few ideas to add, and now we have so many great things to try. Rocks, water, sand, soil—here, I've got a whole list written down."

Pip looked over what I'd written and scratched his head. "So how will this tell us where our plant is from again?"

"If we can figure out what our seeds grow best in, that will give us a big clue. Like if the seeds start growing on rocks, we know the pod probably came from the top of one of the mountains, or any other place around here that has a lot of rocks all in one spot."

Pip nodded. "Oh, now I get it. So first we need to try all these things, and then we'll use that answer to figure out where we should take the pod!"

"Exactly! I want to get these seeds back to the right place right away. I don't know if they're going to do something weird like dry out, or I don't even know what. So let's get cracking!" I grabbed my science journal and a pen and started writing as I spoke. "First, we start with our question."

QUESTION: What will our mystery seeds grow in?

"And next is our hypothesis. So here is where we make a guess. What do you think, Pip? Where will our mystery seeds grow?"

"Hmm." Pip tapped his chin. "I think the mystery seeds will grow in water. Because the seed pod looks like a merhorse stone, and those are usually underwater."

"Ooh, great guess, Pip!" I wrote down his guess and then added mine.

HYPOTHESIS:

(Zoey) I think the mystery seeds will grow in potting soil because that's where most of the plants I know of grow.

"OK, now we need to figure out all the materials we need."

"You said sand, water, rocks, and ... I don't remember the others." Pip shrugged.

"Oh, and soil and that mix of sand and moss Mom told me to try. Here we go ..."

MATERIALS: Cups, dirt from our yard, potting soil, stream water, sand, sand/moss mix, rocks, mystery seeds, labels, and marker

I tapped my pencil on my lip. "How many seeds do we have?"

Pip carefully counted and announced, "Twenty-four!"

"OK, perfect. We want to try six different ways to grow them ... so with twenty-four seeds ... we can put four seeds in each container!"

Pip made six little piles of four seeds each.

"OK, I can get pots and labels from inside, potting soil from the greenhouse, rocks from our driveway, stream water from the stream ..."

"But what about sand?" Pip asked. "And moss?"

"Hmm, Mom said peat moss would be the best to try. But I forgot to ask her where to find that."

Pip gave a joyful jump. "I know where to find that moss in the forest. I can also get the stream water!"

"Perfect! Now we just need to figure out where to find sand . . ."

Sassafras went running for the barn door. He stopped at the door and looked over his shoulder and gave an annoyed meow.

"Oh! You want me to follow you."

Sassafras led the way out to my sandbox. "Brilliant! Good kitty!" I scratched under his chin and he purred. "Wait here. I'll be right back with the cups."

Several minutes later, Pip, Sassafras, and I met up in the barn.

Pip panted in front of a small pile of moss and a bit of stream water. "Now what?"

"Now we write out our steps. In an experiment it's important to change just one thing and keep everything else . . ."

" . . . the same!" chirped Pip. "Your mom is always saying that."

I laughed and nodded. "She is! We're

changing the stuff we are trying to grow the seeds in. So we should use the same pots, the same number of seeds in each pot, and the same amount of stuff in each pot. We should also keep them in the same place. And I'm pretty sure all seeds need water to grow, so I'll add the same small amount of water to each of them."

PROCEDURE:

1. Get six plastic pots and label each (yard dirt, potting soil, stream water, sand, sand/moss mix, and rocks).

2. Fill each pot halfway with the material.

3. Place four seeds in a square shape in each cup.

4. Add one teaspoon of water to each cup.

5. Check on seeds every day.

33

With Pip and Sassafras both helping, we got through the seed planting pretty quickly. As we stood back to admire our work, Pip let out a monstrous yawn.

"I think my work here is done. Time for a nap! I'll see you tomorrow."

Sassafras and I gave Pip a quick snuggle. "See you tomorrow, Pip!"

CHAPTER 6
NOTHING?!

Sassafras and I rushed through breakfast and out to the barn first thing the next morning.

"Which pots do you think will have sprouted seeds, Sassafras?" I asked as I peeked in the ones filled with rocks, dirt, and air.

Sassafras gave a few sniffs at the pots in front of him before plopping down with a worried look on his face.

"None of those sprouted either, Sass?"

I peeked in to double-check, but the seeds all looked pretty much the same.

The doorbell rang, and Sassafras perked up.

"It's probably Pip." We jogged over to the back barn door and sure enough, there was our froggy friend.

"Did any grow?" Pip asked hopefully.

"Nope. Nothing's changed." I shrugged. "Sometimes we have to wait a few days before our pea and bean seeds sprout."

Pip tapped his chin. "Hmmm. That could be, but usually magical plants grow quickly. Because of the magic and all."

"Really? That's not good. I must be missing something or doing something wrong! But what?" I paced back and forth. Sassafras bonked into my leg.

"Mrrph."

I looked down, and Sassafras had my Thinking Goggles in his mouth. "Oh, great idea!" I plunked the goggles on my head.

I paced some more while I waited for

the Thinking Goggles to work.

I started tapping my legs a little as I walked.

"Of course!" I exclaimed. "The pod didn't open until I sang. Maybe the seeds need music to grow? Ummm, let's see here." I hummed to get myself started.

Seeds, seeds, why won't you grow?
This whole thing is going too slow.

I started to dance a bit and bonked my

arm into the bookcase.

Ouch! I just bopped my right elbow.

Pip squealed. "Zoey! The seeds are doing something—keep singing!"

Ummm, gee, I wish I had a banjo.
Why don't you come out and say hello?
'Cause if you did we'd all say "Whoa!"

At that, we saw some of the seeds shake a little, and the shiny black outsides began to crack. As my song promised, we all said, "Whoa!"

Well, except for Sass, who said "Meow!"

"Sing more, Zoey! It's working!" exclaimed Pip.

I tried thinking of more words to sing, but I couldn't. So I put my head next to Pip's and we both sang my original song again. As we sang, the seeds moved and shook a bit more. Maybe the roots were starting to grow? Whatever was going on, it was happening very gradually.

"I can't sing all day, Pip. There must be

a better way to . . . OH! Of course! A radio!"

I grabbed it from the cabinet, set it up by the plants, and turned on my favorite radio station. By dinnertime each of the seeds had grown a few inches. The seeds in the rocks, dirt, and potting soil pots had grown the smallest amount, and the seeds in the sand, sand mixed with moss, and water had grown the most. I had just finished writing down the measurements in my journal when Mom called me in for dinner.

DATA:

STUFF	HEIGHT (INCHES)
yard dirt	4 inches
potting sail	4 inches
stream water	6 inches
sand	5 inches
sand/ moss mix	6 inches
Rocks	3 inches

"I'm just going to leave the radio on low all night. Can you meet us again first thing tomorrow, Pip?"

He nodded, and we said our goodbyes. I grinned. The plants would be huge tomorrow! And the best part was, it looked like they could maybe grow anywhere. Maybe we could plant them by our house. That would be so neat.

I sang quietly as I shut the barn door for the night:

Oh, plants, plants, good night!
I'll see you in the morning light.
I hope you will be quite the sight!

CHAPTER 7
OH NO!

Following our usual routine, Sassafras and I burst into the barn right after breakfast, full of excitement.

"I bet they are going to be enormous, Sass!" I skipped over to the table and skidded to a stop.

"Oh no!!!" I gasped.

The pots with rocks, potting soil, and yard dirt looked completely empty. I stepped closer. Where there had been plants, there was now nothing but . . .

purple ashes? All the plants in those pots were dead.

My lip quivered. My stomach tightened. "We need Mom!"

Sassafras and I dashed back to the house. I wiped my tears so Dad wouldn't worry. He couldn't see anything magical, and I couldn't explain what was wrong without talking about a magical seed pod. Dad would be so confused.

I took a few deep breaths to steady myself, and then went straight to Mom's office.

She took one look at me and opened her arms. "Oh honey, what's wrong?"

The tears started again.

"It's about the seeds. Pip and Sassafras and I

discovered that music helped them grow last night and they were all doing great . . ."

"Right—you showed me your data, and it was all great. Did they stop growing?"

"Worse! The plants in three of the containers are completely dead. All that's left in the pots are purple ashes."

Mom was confused by this, too, so she came out to the barn and took a look herself.

"How strange! These must be very delicate magical plants. You did a great job—there was no way we could have known they would turn to ashes like that. I would have done the same things you did."

I sniffled. That did make me feel better. But still, I only had twelve plants left. If these were the last twelve of their kind, I needed to be extra super-duper careful. I didn't want to be the one to make such a beautiful and rare magical plant go extinct.

"We can talk through the rest of your

plans together and make sure we're being careful with the seeds we have left. Let's start with what you learned here." Mom scooted a ruler and my science journal over to me.

I carefully measured the plants we had left and added the information to my data chart.

DATA:

STUFF	HEIGHT(INCHES)	HEIGHT(INCHES)
yard dirt	4 inches	———
potting soil	4 inches	—
stream water	6 inches	8 inches
sand	5 inches	7 inches
sand/moss mix	6 inches	18 inches
Rocks	3 inches	

Then I spoke as I wrote:

CONCLUSION:

The mystery seeds grow ~~best~~ tallest in sand mixed with moss. They sort of grow in water and sort of in sand. They do NOT grow in rocks, yard dirt, or potting soil.

Also PS they need music or songs to grow.

"Perfect," said Mom. "What are you planning to do next?"

"Because the plants are so much taller in the sand-and-moss mix, I think I should move the plants in water and sand into pots with sand and moss. And then the next thing I need to figure out is how much to water them."

Mom nodded. "And you have a bit of a clue there about the water…"

I tapped my Thinking Goggles. "I know that the amount of water I gave them to start was maybe OK, since the plants in sand and moss are still growing."

"Mmmm-hmmm," said Mom. "And one more thing … ?"

"Ummm …"

Pip cleared his throat near the pot of plants in water.

"OH! Thanks, Pip! Having a lot of water is probably OK, since those plants are growing all right."

Pip and Mom clapped, and I grinned.

Mom gave my shoulders a squeeze. "Sounds like you're ready for your next experiment."

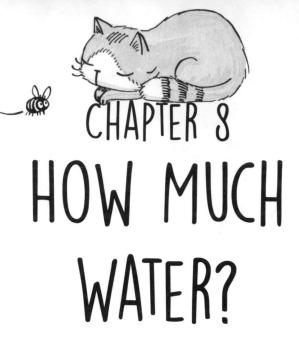

CHAPTER 8

HOW MUCH WATER?

The plants were getting crowded with four per pot, so I very, very carefully separated them out and gave each plant its own pot filled halfway with sand and moss mixed together. Pip had helped gather more peat moss from the forest before going home for the day.

I hummed along to the radio and sat down with my science journal. I started with the new question:

QUESTION: How much
water will make the
mystery plants grow the
best?

I thought for a minute. Oh right. Ugh.
I scratched out "best." If Mom were here,
she'd say: *What does best mean? Tallest?
Widest? Most leaves? Be specific, Zoey!*

I fixed my journal entry:

QUESTION: How much
water will make the
mystery plants grow the
~~best~~ tallest?

And then I got to make a guess. Aw,
man! I should've asked Pip for his guess
before he left. Oh well.

"All right, Sassafras. We've learned
that, um ..." I flipped back in my science

49

journal. " . . . the best amount of water is probably between one teaspoon and half a pot of water."

Sassafras blinked lazily at me, and then laid his head down and started to snore.

Well then. I guess I'd need to write in my journal quietly.

HYPOTHESIS:
I think five teaspoons of water will make the mystery plant grow the tallest.

I checked to make sure all my materials were on the table—water, teaspoons, twelve pots with plants. Check, check, check!

OK, on to the procedure. How much water should I try in each? I did NOT want to wake up to more purple ashes tomorrow.

I quietly labeled my pots and then drew out my plan while Sassafras snored.

PROCEDURE:

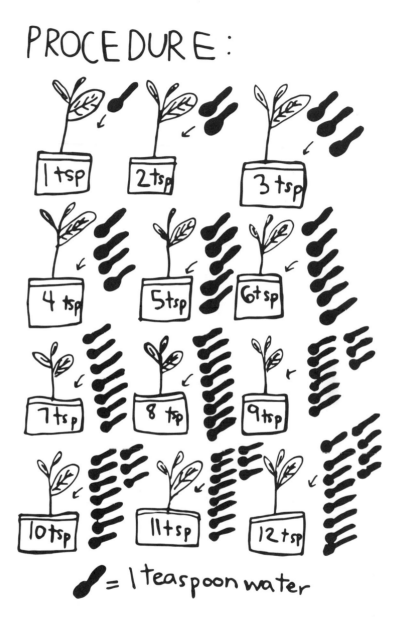

= 1 teaspoon water

I started singing again (quietly) as I added the water. It couldn't hurt.

One for you,
And two now too.
Three will do.
And four—who knew?
Doo doo doo doo doo
doo doooooo
Almost through,
Now twelve—
woohoo!

Sassafras yawned and stretched. Then he looked at my closed journal and the labeled pots and gave a little jump.

"I finished it all while you slept. Our little plants should be fine now. I hope. Let's go tell Mom and make sure my experiment sounds OK."

I crossed my fingers and my toes as I closed the barn door.

"Pleeeeease be OK, little plants!" I whispered.

CHAPTER 9
NOT AGAIN!

I woke up the next morning full of hope, but when we got to the barn, my shoulders slumped. Three more plants had turned to ashes.

Mom rubbed my back. "It's not your fault, honey! This is a tricky problem and a delicate plant. Which three did we lose overnight?"

"The plants in the pots that got one, two, and twelve teaspoons of water." My stomach felt like I'd swallowed a rock.

"But look! Now we know more about your plant . . ." Mom gestured to the growing plants.

I took a deep breath to try to calm myself down. Panicking wouldn't help the nine plants that were left. I grabbed my ruler with a shaky hand and measured. "OK, so it looks like the six-teaspoon plant has grown the most. That must be close to the perfect amount of water." I poked a finger in the soil. "It's kind of mushy and

wet. That's strange, right?"

"It is unusual." Mom seemed to be waiting for me to figure it out.

I could do this. "OK, so we know that it likes sand mixed with moss. And that it likes to be a little soggy. Soggy . . . soggy . . . OH! Boggy! It's that thing you were telling me about when I started, right? A bog?"

Mom smiled. "Exactly. Remember, a bog is a kind of wetland. The plants there are used to soils that are similar to a sand-and-moss mix, and they're usually OK with a bit of standing water. I agree with your conclusion that our mystery plants seem to want to grow in a bog."

I peeked out the barn window into the forest. "And you said there's one around here?"

Mom pointed off in the distance. "The one I know of is a few miles that way, but there aren't any roads to it. The only way to get there is a pretty steep and long hike."

"I love hiking!" I flexed my arm

muscles. "And I'm tough. Can I come with you to take the plants back? Please, Mom?" I was super excited to get the plants back where they belonged. And I was a little worried that the longer I kept them, the more likely I would wake up to more purple ashes.

Mom laughed. "You are tough. I have to go into work today, but maybe we can go tomorrow."

"YESSS!" I jumped up and down.

"Why don't you get all of these plants watered for the day, and then you and Sassafras can start packing everything we'll need for a long day hike—hats and bug spray and snacks and all that?"

"We're on it!"

CHAPTER 10
SURPRISE!

Sassafras and I had just finished packing two backpacks—mainly full of yummy snacks—when we heard the magic doorbell ring.

"I think it's Pip. He was supposed to come this morning, but all those trips back and forth with the peat moss and stream water must have really tired him out."

Sassafras and I ran for the barn.

We opened the door to find a smiley Pip.

"What did I miss?" He asked as he hopped onto my head. Oh, Pip.

I swallowed and then broke the bad news. "We lost three more plants. But we learned that the plants grow the tallest with six teaspoons of water a day. And see . . ." I squished the wet soil with my finger again. "We're almost positive they're bog plants!"

"Oooooh!" Pip cooed.

"I know, the soggy soil is pretty cool, right?"

"No. I mean yes. But oooooh, look at those!"

I couldn't tell what Pip was so excited about, so I plucked him down from my head. He pointed up to the top of the plants.

"Oh my goodness! How did we not see those? Sassafras! Look!"

I picked up Sassafras, Pip jumped back on my head, and we crowded around what looked like sparkling flower buds.

"I can't wait to see the flowers. They

must be amazing! Can you even imagine?"

"How do we get them to bloom?" asked Pip.

"Um, well ... that's a great question. Flowers usually bloom in the spring and summer when it's warm and sunny. So these guys probably just need some sun!"

"Ohhh!" Pip gently touched a low-hanging flower bud with one webbed hand. "Do you think they will bloom right away if we take them outside now?"

"That's a great idea! Maybe we can surprise my mom with the

flowers! She's at work today but she'll be home later."

One by one, I moved the seven plants out into the sunshine.

"I'm putting them here by this tree because see?" I pointed up. "There are lots of bees! And bees pollinate flowers."

Pip gave me a puzzled look. "Pollinate?"

"Yeah, flowers need pollen added from other flowers to grow a fruit or a seed pod."

Pip coughed a little. "Um, pollen?"

I spotted a dandelion and plucked it. "A bee lands on a flower to get some food." I tapped the dandelion against the palm of my hand and showed Pip the yellow dust left behind. "When she lands, some of this pollen dust will get on her little feet. When she goes to another flower for more food, she'll leave some of the pollen on that new flower and pick up some more."

Pip poked at the pollen in my hand.

I scanned the yard and ran over to pick a dandelion that was white and puffy with seeds. "The pollen the bees leave makes it so the flower can turn into a seed or seeds like this!" I blew and all the little dandelion seeds rained down on Pip's head as he giggled.

"Ooh! So maybe we just need bees! And

then our flowers will make more rainbow seed pods," exclaimed Pip.

"Yes! And then our plant won't go extinct." I cheered. We high-fived.

Pip and I lay in the grass and propped our heads on our elbows as we watched.

And waited.

And watched.

Nothing happened.

"Maybe we need some music? I can't bring the radio all the way out, but I could turn it up."

I ran back into the barn and turned the radio louder. I walked back outside to check. We could definitely hear it.

More watching.
More waiting.
More nothing.

Pip yawned. "Um, Zoey? This is getting a little boring. It's such a pretty day. Could we take a break and go visit the merhorses? Pretty please?"

I didn't want to miss the flowers blooming ... but it didn't look like it was going to happen anytime soon. I hadn't seen the merhorses in a while. And Pip was here to translate for me (it was really hard to say much to the merhorses without Pip there since I couldn't understand

anything they said back to me).

Just then Dad came out into the yard. "What're you doing with those empty pots, sweetie?"

I giggled. "A science experiment with plants. Hey, Dad? Can I go down to the stream for a little while? I'll be back by dinnertime."

Dad stared at the pots for one more moment, and then patted me on the head. "Sure!"

I stood up and gave him a quick hug. "Thanks, Dad!"

Pip hopped onto my head, Sassafras ran ahead, and we all set off for the stream.

CHAPTER 11
ONLY TWO

I grinned as I tickled the baby merhorse under the chin. I thought nothing could be cuter than merhorses . . . but baby merhorses? Yep, pretty much the most adorable thing ever.

Sassafras was peeking at the little one in the water from his perch on a fallen log (as much as he loved merhorses, there was no way he wanted to get wet!) and his ears started twitching. Then his head snapped toward home.

I strained to hear my mom calling my name.

"Sorry, merhorses! It was so much fun playing with you, but I've got to go. We'll visit again soon!"

Pip hopped on my head and I lifted Sassafras into my arms and hauled them both to the other side of the stream.

"I can't wait to show Mom the flowers. Do you think they've bloomed? It's been

longer than I thought if Mom is already home from work. Let's hurry!"

We ran the whole way, and as soon as we made it into the yard I could tell that something was wrong. My mom was not smiling like usual. Instead she looked really sad.

"Mom!" I puffed, slightly out of breath from running. "What's ... wrong?"

Mom opened her mouth, then closed it. She opened it once more, then sighed. "There's just not an easy way to tell you. I'm sorry, but there are only two plants left."

Pip and I both gasped.

"But ... how?" I looked over to the tree where we'd left the plants, but they weren't there. "Wait! Where are they?"

Mom put her arm around me and we started walking together to the barn. "When I got home, I went over to see if I could figure out why you had moved them outside, and I noticed that seven of the plants had turned to ashes. The only two that were left were shaded by the tree's shadow. I rushed them back into the barn. I think they can't handle full sun, honey."

A tear rolled down my face. "We should never have left them. We shouldn't have gone to the stream! We only have two left?"

Mom wiped my tear away. "They're fine for now. There are even some flower buds, which is exciting! We just have to keep trying our best."

"But what if the bog you're thinking of

isn't the right place? What if I do something else wrong and the last two plants turn to ashes? I don't want the plants to die!" I didn't want to say my biggest worry out loud, but I couldn't hold it in anymore.

With a big sob I blurted, "What if I'm the one who makes this plant go extinct?!"

"Oh, sweetheart! Magical plants are rare, but I would be really surprised if this was the last of its kind ever. Let's focus on our plan and hope that bog is the right one. And even though we lost plants today, now we know something new, right?"

I nodded sadly. "Yeah, we know not to plant them in the sun. We'll need to find a place that's shaded."

"You still look like you need some cheering up. How about a picnic dinner with Dad? I picked up some of your favorite things to eat at the store—we can set up a feast!"

I sniffed. "Thanks, Mom. Can Pip join us?"

Pip huffed. "I highly doubt you'd have

anything I'd find delicious on the menu. Human food is so gross! And besides, I'd better get my rest. We have a big hike tomorrow."

I clapped my hands together. "You're coming on the hike with us?"

"Wouldn't miss it!" said Pip. He gave us all good-night hugs and headed off into the forest, calling out, "See you tomorrow!" as he hopped away.

CHAPTER 12
WHAT'S THAT SMELL?

Mom, Dad, Sassafras, and I were all enjoying our picnic dinner. Mom had even picked up a can of tuna fish for Sassafras, and he was savoring each bite as he purred loudly.

A warm breeze ruffled my hair.

It was such a beautiful night and the food was so delicious that I actually started to feel a little better. Maybe those two plants weren't the last of their kind. And now I knew not to plant them in the sun at the bog. Maybe those flower buds would get pollinated and turn into a bunch of rainbow seed pods after all. Hopeful for tomorrow's hike, I made a silent wish that everything would work out.

I took a deep breath to try to let go of some of my worries. Wait a minute. I sniffed. Something smelled amazing.

Mom, Dad, and Sassafras must have noticed the smell, too, because they stopped eating and started sniffing the air.

"What is that incredible smell?" asked Dad.

"I'm not sure," answered Mom. She sniffed some more.

"It smells like roses and lilacs and honeysuckle all blooming at once." I sighed, and then sniffed some more. "Can Sassafras and I go find out where it's coming from?"

Mom and Dad nodded their approval. Sassafras looked at me, then his tuna, then me, then his tuna. Finally he gave a big sigh, gobbled a giant mouthful of tuna, and trotted over to me.

We walked around our house and through the garden, but we couldn't figure out the source of the smell.

"Where is it coming from, Sass?"

Sassafras gulped the last of the tuna in his mouth and sat for a second. He sniffed first one way, then the other, spinning around in a complete circle. Then his eyes lit up, and he started chattering and took off for the barn.

The barn? OH!! THE BARN! I ran after him.

I threw open the barn door and turned on the light.

"Woooooowwwwww," I breathed. Sassafras started purring. There in front of us were several of the most beautiful flowers I'd ever seen.

"They're beautiful," I murmured. "We have to tell Mom!"

We ran back to the picnic blanket and I blurted out, "You have to come see! In the barn!!!" before I remembered. My dad can't

see magical creatures. Or plants. Whoops.

Mom's eyes got really big, but she answered, "Oh, the smell is coming from the barn? How unusual! Sure, we can come check it out!"

She gave me a wink as she and Dad got up and followed us to the barn.

Inside, Mom couldn't seem to help exclaiming, "Oh my goodness!" The flowers really were so breathtaking!

Dad looked around puzzled. "You're

right, hon, this really is so strange! It smells so wonderful in here, but the only thing I see are these pots of sand and . . . moss? Are you trying to grow something, Zoey?"

I did my best not to laugh. Poor Dad! All he could see were the soil cups. I really wished he could see the flowers too. At least he got to smell the amazing smell. It was a start!

"I sure am, Dad."

"Well, keep at it. I'm sure something will grow for you eventually."

Mom coughed to cover her laugh. It was so funny to hear Dad saying this in front of these enormous plants covered with gorgeous flowers. Oh, Dad.

Hey, wait a minute. It was kind of weird that the flowers didn't bloom until the night. "Um, Mom? Just out of curiosity, are there plants that only flower at night? Or do most plants start blooming at night and I just haven't noticed?"

Mom smiled. "What a great question! Some plants only bloom during the day, and some only at night. Some bloom both day and night. The flowers are meant to attract their perfect pollinators, so you can get clues about who that pollinator might be by looking at the flower. For instance, a flower that smells like rotting meat and garbage is probably pollinated by a fly. And a flower that only opens at night

is probably pollinated by a nocturnal creature—something only awake at night."

"Wait, what? I thought only bees pollinated plants?"

Dad jumped in. "Ooh! I know the answer to this one. There are actually lots of different creatures that can pollinate plants. Birds and butterflies are great pollinators. So are monkeys, lizards, bats, beetles, ants, and even your favorites—mosquitoes!"

I shivered. "Ew, mosquitoes are pollinators?"

Dad laughed. "Yep, there are some endangered orchids that rely on mosquitoes to pollinate them."

"Weeeeeird."

Mom looked at Dad. "Hey, honey? What if instead of going on a day hike tomorrow, Zoey and I camp overnight? She might be, uh, able to see some nighttime pollinators up close." Mom winked at me again.

I crossed my fingers. The only thing

more
exciting
than a hike
would be a
hike AND
camping
overnight.
Dad
thought for a
minute. "That's
a great idea! The weather should be nice. I
might be able to come with you, but I have
that big project from work . . ."

"Why don't you take a quiet evening at
home," Mom said. "We'll be just fine."

"As long as you don't mind?"

"We'll be great, Dad!" Mom and I
quietly high-fived.

CHAPTER 13

CAMPING!

I held my breath as I opened the barn door the next morning.

"Oh, thank goodness! They are OK, Sassafras. Oh, and look! The flowers are closed again. Mom is on to something with that whole nighttime pollinator thing."

Sassafras meowed in agreement.

"Do you think the pollinator will be some kind of giant magical moth? I loooove moths!"

Sassafras chattered excitedly.

"ARGH! No eating the pollinators, Sassafras."

I gave each plant its six teaspoons of water, and then Pip hopped in through the open barn door.

"Everyone ready for the hike?" Pip asked. "Wait, where's your mom?"

I explained about our discovery the night before and bounced up and down a little when I got to the part about getting to camp overnight at the bog. "Pleeeeease say you'll come camp with us?"

Sassafras bumped Pip gently with his head.

"Ohhh, all right, you two. I'll go."

"Mom says we should meet back here at one o'clock."

"One o'clock it is!" Pip declared. "I just have to hop home and pack."

Sassafras and I spent the morning inside setting up more pea plant experiments. In all the excitement about the magical plant, I'd forgotten about the colored leaves experiments I wanted to start.

At long last, it was time to leave. Mom, Sassafras, and I arrived at the barn to find Pip wearing a tiny frog-sized backpack.

"Ready to go!" he announced and hopped up onto my mom's head.

Mom laughed. "I'll carry the frog and the backpack and one of the plants. Can you carry the other plant, Zoey? And Sassafras, you can walk?"

We set off on our long, long, long hike. It was really tiring having to carry a large plant AND hike. I was trying hard not to be too grumbly ... and not being too successful ... when Mom finally declared that we'd arrived.

I carefully set down the plant in the shade and took a look around. The bog looked really cool, but I didn't see any plants that looked like ours.

I squished my fingers in some soil I found in the shade, though. "This squishes just right, Mom. Should we plant them or should we leave them in the pots until we know for sure this is the right place?"

Mom sat down and sighed. "Well, they're getting too big for their pots as it is. I don't know of any other bogs nearby, so let's just be hopeful and try planting them here."

I dug a big juicy hole in the sandy and mucky bog soil. I closed my eyes and whispered a wish that this was the right place and the right thing to do. Then I gently removed the first magical plant from the pot and placed it in the bog.

I squished the soggy soil back around the roots.

Once it was solidly in the hole, the plant grew almost instantly about an inch in every direction.

"Did you see that?" Pip yelped.

"I did!" Mom exclaimed. "I think that's a promising sign! Let's keep our fingers crossed."

I planted the second plant, and it did the same little growth spurt, then nothing.

Mom handed me a bottle of water to clean my hands, and we settled down for an early dinner. After all that hiking and plant carrying, I was starving.

Sassafras chattered hungrily, and I patted his head. "Remember—no eating moths or any other buggy creature that might be the magical plant pollinator."

Sassafras meowed in agreement, and I opened a can of tuna to the sound of rumbly cat purrs. Pip hopped off into the forest to find a froggy snack.

After we'd eaten, we just sat and stared at the plants. The sun was starting to think about setting. I was hoping once it was dark out, the flowers would bloom again and the pollinators would be able to follow the flower scent to find the magical plants.

"Waiting can be kind of boring, I know," said Mom. "So I thought I'd bring a little something." She dropped a bag of marshmallows on my lap.

I perked up. "S'mores? YES!!!!!"

We roasted marshmallows as the sun finally set. "Do you think we'll ever see baby Marshmallow again?" I asked.

"Well, I'm sure he's hardly a baby anymore. And dragons tend to just stick with each other. They don't often interact with humans. You were pretty lucky to get to meet him. He was the first baby dragon I'd ever met, and I've been helping at the barn for most of my life."

I sighed. "Yeah, that makes sense."

Pip was staring at the plants. "Do the flowers seem to sparkle a bit more out here?"

Mom nodded. "I noticed that too."

"Meow! Meow!" Sassafras interrupted.

Mom, Pip, and I turned to him. His ears were doing the weird twitchy thing they do when he hears something interesting.

Very faintly, I could just make out a "lalalalalalalalala." I had never met a fairy, but I imagined this was what one would sound like.

"Fairies?" I whispered.

Mom's eyes lit up. She jumped to her
feet.

Pip hopped up and down and cheered.
"Fweeps!"

I followed their gazes and saw dozens
of floating furry shapes. They looked like
they were swimming through the air. They
reminded me of the dancing sea slugs,
nudibranchs, that I loved watching at the
aquarium. But these magical creatures

were furry and sparkly. And they sang!

Several of the fweeps circled my mom, their sparkly fur rippling gracefully in the air. One landed on her shoulder. One landed on her hand. They nuzzled her cheeks.

Mom knelt down. "Oh, Zoey. These are my little friends, the fweeps. I got to help them many years ago."

I reached out to touch them. They were

so so soft. "I remember! From your science journal!"

Just then the fweeps' song got even faster and they swam-flew through the air to the magical plants.

"Look, Mom! I think they are the magical plant's pollinator!"

We tiptoed over and watched. As the fweeps sang, the plants grew, and more buds opened. Of course! Their songs made the plants grow even better than mine (or the radio's). The fweeps carefully landed on each blossom. It sounded like they were eating something from the flower. Maybe some sweet nectar at the back? And each time a fweep landed on a flower, you could see something sparkly like glitter on their fur.

Pip proudly pointed, "Look, Zoey—pollen!"

Mom and I nodded in agreement.

After the fweeps visited every flower on each plant, they swirled around all of us once more. Then just as quickly as they'd appeared, they left.

Sassafras meowed, and Mom, Pip, and I turned. He was staring at one of the flowers. As we watched, the flower petals slowly shriveled as the bottom part of the flower swelled and grew.

"Whaaat?" I started to ask.

"Shhh, just watch," Mom said with a smile.

The bottom part of the flower grew and grew. And as it grew, it started to glow.

First red, then orange, then . . .

"MOM! NEW SEED PODS! We did it!
We saved the magical plant!"

Pip and Sassafras jumped in my arms,
and Mom hugged us all. "You sure did,
baby!"

CHAPTER 14

A PHOTO?

The next morning we woke up early to the sounds of the birds in the forest. I held my breath, slowly unzipped the tent door, and stepped out.

The plants were still there. They were still huge. There were still a few new closed flowers. And there were a ton of glowing seed pods lying on the ground near each plant.

I let out a big sigh of relief.

Mom came out of the tent, and we cuddled together, eating some warm oatmeal while we watched the beautiful rainbow show of the new seed pods.

"So . . . we have to leave them all here, right? I mean, this is where they belong. So it's what's best?"

Mom nodded. "I know it's hard to leave them. Now that we know where the plants grow, though, we can come camp again sometime soon. Maybe even bring your dad?"

"That's true. I bet Dad would love it here, even if he can't see the fweeps or the beautiful plants."

"And there's one other thing you could do to make saying goodbye a little easier."

I raised one of my eyebrows.

"Check in the backpack toward the bottom."

I ran over and dug through the backpack. My hand closed around . . . my camera!

"Yessss! Thank you, Mom!" I knelt down to get a close-up photo of a rainbow seed pod that had already fallen on the ground.

"How about I take your photo with one,

sweetie?"

"Oooh! That would be even cooler!"

Sassafras let out a long and fussy meow, and Pip humphed.

"Sorry, guys! Of course you should be in the photo." Pip leaped onto my head and I snuggled up to Sassafras.

"Say cheese!" Mom said. Sassafras purred, and Pip and I grinned at the camera.

When we got home, I went straight to my room and added the photo to my science journal. Sassafras, Pip, and I looked frozen in time in the photo, but the seed pod glowed out from the photo in rainbow colors. "Cooooooool," I breathed.

Just opposite the shimmering rainbow photo was a blank page, ready and waiting for whoever we would meet next.

GLOSSARY

Bog: A wet place with lots of mud and usually standing water.

Pollinate: When pollen from one part of a flower is added to another part of a flower. A flower must be pollinated to grow a fruit.

Pollinator: Whatever thing moves the pollen grains from one part of a flower to another.

Seed pod: A shell or cover that protects a plant's seeds. Not all plants have seed pods around their seeds.

Species: A group of creatures or plants that share common features.

Sprout: When a seed starts growing.

ABOUT THE AUTHOR AND ILLUSTRATOR

ASIA CITRO used to be a science teacher, but now she plays at home with her two kids and writes books. When she was little, she had a cat just like Sassafras. He loved to eat bugs and always made her laugh (his favorite toy was a plastic human nose that he carried everywhere). Asia has also written three activity books: *150+ Screen-Free Activities for Kids, The Curious Kid's Science Book,* and *A Little Bit of Dirt.* She has yet to find a baby dragon in her backyard, but she always keeps an eye out, just in case.

MARION LINDSAY is a children's book illustrator who loves stories and knows a good one when she reads it. She likes to draw anything and everything but does spend a completely unfair amount of time drawing cats. Sometimes she has to draw dogs just to make up for it. She illustrates picture books and chapter books as well as painting paintings and designing patterns. Like Asia, Marion is always on the lookout for dragons and sometimes thinks there might be a small one living in the airing cupboard.

for activities and more visit
ZOEYANDSASSAFRAS.COM